W9-BQS-283

38709 00694826 6

Madison High School
Media Center

Great Ideas of Science

CLASSIFICATION OF LIFE

by Melissa Stewart

Twenty-First Century Books
Minneapolis

Text copyright © 2008 by Melissa Stewart

All rights reserved. International copyright secured. No part of this book may be reproduced, stored in a retrieval system, or transmitted in any form or by any means—electronic, mechanical, photocopying, recording, or otherwise—without the prior written permission of Lerner Publishing Group, Inc., except for the inclusion of brief quotations in an acknowledged review.

Twenty-First Century Books
A division of Lerner Publishing Group, Inc.
241 First Avenue North
Minneapolis, MN 55401 U.S.A.

Website address: www.lernerbooks.com

Library of Congress Cataloging-in-Publication Data

Stewart, Melissa.
    Classification of life / by Melissa Stewart.
        p.   cm. — (Great ideas of science)
    Includes bibliographical references and index.
    ISBN-13: 978–0–8225–6604–5 (lib. bdg. : alk. paper)
    1. Biology—Classification—Juvenile literature. I. Title.
QH83.S764 2008
578.01'2—dc22   2006028533

Manufactured in the United States of America
1 2 3 4 5 6 – DP – 13 12 11 10 09 08

TABLE OF CONTENTS

INTRODUCTION

DISCOVERING A NEW MONKEY

In 2004 tourists spotted a group of rare monkeys at Udzungwa Mountains National Park in Tanzania. When wildlife biologist Trevor Jones heard that the tourists had seen Sanje mangabeys, he was excited. Even though he'd seen this kind of monkey before, he decided to go take a look.

Jones slowly scanned the mountain forest with his binoculars, looking for gray monkeys with pink faces. He listened carefully for the Sanje mangabey's call, a loud whoop-gobble.

Jones didn't see any Sanje mangabeys that day. Instead, he saw monkeys with brown fur and dark faces. These monkeys called to one another with soft honk-barks. No one had ever seen monkeys like this before. And scientists hadn't discovered a new kind, or species, of monkey in Africa in more than twenty years. "I was gobsmacked," Jones later told reporters.

At around the same time, just 350 miles (563 kilometers)

away, a scientist named Tim Davenport spotted another group of the same monkeys. When Jones and Davenport realized that they were studying the same monkeys, they started working together. In just a few months, they wrote a report describing the new monkey to the world. Their report appeared in the journal *Science* on May 20, 2005.

This newfound monkey wasn't the only species scientists described for the first time in 2005. They also announced the discovery of a new rodent in Laos, two new lemurs in Madagascar, and a new catlike animal in Borneo. The list goes on and on. Each year scientists discover about fifteen thousand species of living things. Most of them are smaller than a bumblebee, but a few are as big as a deer or a monkey.

So far scientists have identified about 1.7 million different species. But some experts believe that as many as 100 million species may share our planet. How do we keep track of so many organisms (living things)? Scientists classify organisms, or sort them into groups, based on their similarities and differences.

To figure out a newfound organism's proper place among all the species we already know, scientists study its body structure and behavior. If scientists can get a tissue sample, they look at the organism's DNA (deoxyribonucleic acid) too. DNA is a molecule that contains all the instructions a cell needs to carry out the activities that maintain life. Parents pass DNA to their offspring during reproduction.

Jones and Davenport could see that their newfound monkey has a lot in common with all monkeys. It has long arms and legs that are perfect for life in the trees. Its flexible fingers and toes can grasp food easily. It has a large brain and has forward-facing eyes for judging distances accurately. But humans have identified almost three hundred monkey species. Where does this newfound creature fit in?

While observing the monkey from a distance, Jones and Davenport noticed that it was a lot like the mangabey monkeys living nearby. It looked similar and behaved similarly. It lived in the same mountain forests and ate the same kinds of food. So Jones and Davenport decided to classify the newfound monkey as a mangabey. But because it had a unique call and some unique physical traits (spiked hair, long whiskers, and brown fur), the scientists thought the monkey should belong to its own mangabey species. They named it the highland mangabey.

A few months after Jones and Davenport published their report, a farmer accidentally trapped a highland mangabey. After studying it up close and testing its DNA, Davenport realized it wasn't as similar to mangabeys as he'd thought. In fact, its DNA was more like baboon DNA.

The new monkey wasn't a mangabey. But it wasn't a baboon either. Because it was so different from all other known monkeys, Davenport couldn't classify it as a species of any existing monkey group. He had to create a new genus (a group containing one or more species) for the monkey and give it a new name. The kipunji was the first new monkey genus discovered in more than eighty-three years. *Science* published this amazing news on June 2, 2006.

Davenport's experience with kipunjis shows that classifying an animal can be tricky. Imagine you were the first person ever to see a clam, a slug, or a mushroom. Could you figure out how these organisms are related to all the other organisms living on Earth? How would you know which characteristics are important to consider in your decision?

Don't worry if you can't answer these questions. You're in good company. Because life is so diverse and

Scientists discovered that the kipunji was a new genus of monkey after testing its DNA in 2006.

complex, scientists often have trouble deciding how organisms are related. As they learn more about living things, scientists often move organisms from one group to another. Most of these changes involve worms, insects, and other small creatures that weren't studied much in the past. But once in a while, scientists reclassify well-known animals, such as birds, mice, and monkeys.

For as long as humans have lived on Earth, we've wanted to understand the natural world. Giving organisms names and sorting them into groups helps us do that. People started developing systems for classifying living things thousands of years ago. Some of these systems didn't work, so people stopped using them. Others worked fairly well, but they weren't perfect. Over time scientists have improved these systems. But classifying living things is still difficult and time consuming. Scientists are constantly revising and updating the tree of life—a big, complex diagram that shows how all Earth's organisms are related to one another.

As researchers keep identifying newfound species, we'll need to keep reworking our ideas about the relationships among living things. But that's no reason to stop trying to organize the natural world. Like the earliest humans, we too have a deep desire to know and understand the creatures that share our planet.

CHAPTER 1

EARLY EFFORTS TO CLASSIFY ORGANISMS

Aristotle was one of the first people to classify living things. He lived in Greece about 2,300 years ago. Aristotle divided all animals into two main categories: animals with red blood and animals without red blood. His categories roughly match the groups modern scientists call vertebrates (animals with backbones) and invertebrates (animals without backbones).

Aristotle also developed a "ladder of nature." It included eleven different groups: (1) humans, (2) mammals, (3) birds, (4) reptiles and amphibians, (5) fish, (6) octopuses and squid, (7) shellfish, (8) insects and spiders, (9) jellyfish, (10) sponges, and (11) plants. Aristotle sorted about five hundred different organisms into these groups.

Before Aristotle classified an animal, he observed its body structures closely. He also considered its behavior. He knew where it lived, what it ate, and how it reproduced. Once he understood a creature well, he compared it to other animals he'd studied.

Before deciding how to classify sea nettles, a kind of jellyfish, Aristotle wrote: "[Sea nettles] resemble plants in some ways, animals in others. Some can move about like other animals and use their bodies to protect themselves from enemies. On the other hand, their body structure is very different from most other animals." Descriptions such as this fill the pages of *On the Parts of Animals* and *History of Animals*, two of Aristotle's great works.

Historians think Aristotle wrote about plants too, but no copies of his works on plants exist to prove it. Luckily, his student Theophrastus kept track of Aristotle's plant classification ideas. In *History of Plants* and *Inquiry into Plants*, Theophrastus divides plants into three major groups according to size, shape, and growth. He called the groups trees, shrubs, and herbs.

A FLOOD OF NEW IDEAS

For more than one thousand years, Aristotle's and Theophrastus's books were the world's most important sources of information on animal and plant classification. One person who read and appreciated these books was William Turner. This English doctor enjoyed studying plants and birds in his free time. In 1544 Turner published a book discussing Aristotle's work on birds. The book also describes the birds Turner observed in England. It was the first printed book devoted entirely to naming and describing birds.

In 1555 another naturalist and doctor, Frenchman Pierre Belon, published a seven-volume series of books called *The Natural History of Birds*. In these books, Belon compares the skeletons of many different birds. He also compares bird bones to human bones. Belon classifies birds based on their body parts and their habitats (where they live). His groups include waterfowl, wading birds, birds of prey, and perching birds. Modern scientists and bird-watchers still use these categories.

Meanwhile, an Italian doctor named Andrea Cesalpino focused his studies on plants. At that time, doctors and other healers treated most illnesses with herbs. They had to understand the medicinal powers of plants. They also had to be able to find and identify plants. Cesalpino specialized in preparing herbal remedies for a wide range of illnesses.

In 1583 Cesalpino wrote *De plantis* (On Plants), a book that finally replaced Theophrastus's ancient texts. In this book, Cesalpino describes fifteen hundred plant species—almost one thousand more than Theophrastus does. He also introduces a clever method for classifying plants. This method focuses on the size, shape, color, and other characteristics of a plant's fruits and seeds.

Cesalpino's classification method caught the attention of a Swiss doctor named Caspar Bauhin. In 1596 he published *Illustrated Exposition of Plants*, a book that describes and classifies nearly six thousand kinds of plants using a modified version of Cesalpino's method. At that time, most naturalists gave plants and animals long, complicated names that described the organisms' most important features. Bauhin's names were much simpler. He usually used just two words. Unfortunately, the world wasn't ready for such a big change. Even though Bauhin's naming system was much easier to use, naturalists continued to name plants the old way.

A LIFETIME OF CONTRIBUTIONS

John Ray's interest in plants began early in life. After graduating from college in 1648, the English naturalist spent most of his time describing and classifying plants. He collected specimens from all over Europe.

During his lifetime, Ray described more than eighteen thousand kinds of plants. He divided them into two broad groups—monocots and dicots—that we still use. A monocot has a single seed leaf (the first leaf or group of leaves to grow on a plant sprout), narrow leaves with parallel veins, and flower parts occurring in threes or multiples of three. Lilies, orchids, and grasses are monocots. Most other flowering plants are dicots. A dicot has two seed leaves, wide leaves with networks of veins, and flower parts occurring in fours or fives or multiples of four or five.

Later, Ray turned his attention to animals. He published his most important works in the late 1600s and early 1700s. In his books, he suggested that all naturalists around the world use Latin words to name living things. In Ray's time, every educated person could read Latin. Naturalists who lived in different countries and spoke different languages could communicate about organisms more easily if they all had Latin names.

Language wasn't the only problem early naturalists faced. Even people who spoke the same language didn't always agree on common names. For example, the English used the name *robin* to describe a different bird

Monocots, such as the oat plant *(left)*, have narrow leaves with parallel veins. Dicots, such as the hobble-bush *(right)*, have wide leaves with branching veins.

species than the Colonial Americans described when they used *robin*. How could naturalists solve this problem? By introducing two different Latin names. The modern scientific name for the European robin is *Erithacus rubecula*, while the scientific name for the American robin is *Turdus migratorius*.

Sometimes a single plant or animal had so many common names that people from different places didn't know they were talking about the same organism—even if they spoke the same language. The cougar is a perfect example. Modern Americans call this big cat by more than a dozen common names. Depending on where you live, you might call the cougar a puma, a panther, a catamount, a painter, a mountain lion, a mountain screamer, a red tiger, a red lion, a king cat, a fire cat, a ghost walker, or a sneak cat. A conversation about the cougar could get pretty confusing without its scientific name, *Felis concolor.*

Early naturalists who studied insects had an even bigger problem. Many insects had (and still have) different common names at different stages of life. Why? Young insects (larvae) often look quite different from their parents. They eat different foods and may live in different habitats. When people first noticed tiny, colorless creatures at the bottoms of ponds, they collected the wigglers and used them as bait. They had no idea these little larvae would grow into mosquitoes. They didn't know that the squirming, legless maggots they sometimes found on their meat were young houseflies. And they didn't realize that the pale, sluggish mealworms in their flour were young darkling beetles. Modern scientific names help people connect the young and adult forms of insects. *Culex pipiens* is the name for all forms of the northern house mosquito. Houseflies and their maggots are both *Musca domestica. Tenebrio molitor* refers to both yellow mealworms and the darkling beetles they become.

John Ray sat for this portrait in about 1700.

What Is a Species?

John Ray was the first naturalist to use the word *species* to refer to the basic unit of classification. *Species* comes from a Latin word that means "appearance," "sort," or "kind." During Ray's time, naturalists always used physical appearance to classify plants and animals.

When modern scientists classify an animal, they consider not only how it looks but also what it eats, how it finds food, and how it reproduces. Sometimes they look at its internal organs or study its DNA. To classify a plant or a fungus, scientists consider its body structures and behaviors. They also study the molecules in its cells. To classify bacteria and other tiny organisms, researchers study the organisms' DNA and other molecules.

Because appearance plays a smaller role in modern classification, the meaning of *species* has shifted to "kind." A species is a particular kind of living thing, such as a dog, a giraffe, or a tulip. All the members of a species group have many traits in common.

In 1942 a German American scientist named Ernst Mayr added an important idea to our definition of *species*. He said that two creatures should be considered members of the same species only if they can mate and produce healthy offspring. For example, a Yorkshire terrier and a German shepherd look quite different. But scientists classify them both as members of the dog species because they can produce a healthy litter of puppies together. Scientists classify dogs and cats as different species. Neither a Yorkshire terrier nor a German shepherd can mate with a Siamese cat.

Ray did more than propose a universal method for naming organisms. He also suggested a new way of classifying them. Ray's peers and the naturalists before them used just one or two key traits to sort living things into groups. Ray thought it was important to consider many different traits.

When classifying a plant, Ray studied its fruit, flowers, leaves, and roots before assigning it to a category. When classifying a bird, Ray paid close attention to the size and shape of its beak. He also thought carefully about its other body features.

When grouping mammals, reptiles, fish, and insects, Ray considered both the form and the function of various body parts. He believed the big picture was more important than any single feature. Scientists would eventually adopt Ray's classification methods. But like Caspar Bauhin, John Ray was ahead of his time.

The Genius behind the Genus

While John Ray was hard at work in England, Joseph Pitton de Tournefort's reputation as a botanist (a scientist who studies plants) was growing in France. In 1683 he became the director of Jardin des Plantes, a world-famous botanical garden in Paris. One of Tournefort's main duties was to collect plants throughout Europe.

Tournefort published his most important book in 1694. *Elements of Botany* classified more than ten thousand plant species according to the size, position, and appearance of their flower petals. Tournefort clustered the ten thousand species into nearly seven hundred larger, more general groups that he called genera. (The singular form of *genera* is *genus*.)

All the plants in each genus had many traits in common, but they weren't similar enough to be members of the same species. For example, *Iris* is the genus name for one group of flowering plants that grow from bulbs. All irises are monocots with big, showy blossoms. This genus contains more than two hundred species, including the blue flag iris (*Iris versicolor*) and the yellowleaf iris (*Iris chrysophylla*).

By introducing the genus grouping, Tournefort made classification much easier. His idea spread quickly through Europe and influenced a new generation of naturalists.

CHAPTER 2

THE FATHER OF CLASSIFICATION

One of the young people who studied Joseph Pitton de Tournefort's work was Carl Linnaeus, a Swedish naturalist born in 1707. Carl's fascination with plants began when he was a child. His schoolmates teased him and called him the little botanist. While other children played games, Carl explored the countryside and collected plants.

A doctor who taught science at Carl's school noticed his interest in plants. The teacher introduced Carl to Tournefort's classification system. Later, the teacher suggested that Carl study medicine and botany.

In 1727 Linnaeus headed off to Lund University to study botany. But after a disappointing year there, he transferred to Uppsala University. Linnaeus liked his new school much better. It had a large botanical garden and an active community of botanists. Linnaeus soon made some important friends. One of them was a botany professor named Olof Rudbeck.

Linnaeus impressed Rudbeck so much that he hired Linnaeus to tutor his sons. Linnaeus lived with the Rudbeck family and often ate meals with them. Eventually Linnaeus began teaching some of Rudbeck's botany classes.

While Linnaeus was a student at Uppsala, he decided to develop a new system for classifying living things. He later explains in his autobiography, "[I] decided to describe all flowers, put them in new classes, reform the names and families in an entirely novel fashion, something that demanded time and almost did away with sleep." He knew this would be a big job. But he had no idea it would take more than forty years or that it would become the focus of his career.

WHAT IS TAXONOMY?

Carl Linnaeus developed the term taxonomy to describe the process of arranging creatures into his classification system. It comes from two Greek words: *taxis*, which means "arrangement," and *nomiā*, which means "method." Most modern scientists define *taxonomy* a bit differently. They say it's the science of describing, identifying, naming, and classifying living things.

When Linnaeus classified creatures, his main goal was bringing order to the natural world. Modern taxonomy has an even more ambitious goal: to understand how life on Earth has evolved. Knowing an organism's proper place in the tree of life helps us understand how the world's cast of organisms has changed over time.

KINGDOMS, CLASSES, AND MORE

In the early 1730s, Linnaeus visited the wilderness in northern Sweden and Finland. He returned from the journey with hundreds of pressed flowers. He also brought back notebooks full of information about the landscape, the wildlife, the rocks, and the people. Linnaeus's travels fueled his desire to classify living things.

Soon after completing his medical studies, Linnaeus met some wealthy men who were interested in botany. They agreed to pay the publishing costs for Linnaeus's first book. *System of Nature* was just eleven pages long, but it changed the way botanists thought about classifying living things. The 1735 edition provided clear, easy rules for dividing nature into three kingdoms: plants, animals, and minerals. Linnaeus also sorted the members of each kingdom into smaller subgroups based on their physical similarities.

Linnaeus divided the plant kingdom into twenty-four classes. To sort plants into these classes, he studied the number and position of stamens (male reproductive organs)

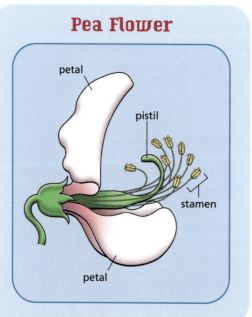

Pea Flower

petal

pistil

stamen

petal

inside their flowers. He divided the animal kingdom into six classes: mammals, birds, amphibians, fish, insects, and worms.

But Linnaeus didn't stop there. Still using physical similarities to guide him, he divided each class of plants and animals into smaller subgroups called orders. Then he divided each order into families, each family into genera, and each genus into species. At each level from kingdom to species, the creatures became more and more similar.

As Linnaeus continued to study the natural world, he revised and updated *System of Nature* twelve times. Later editions focused on just two kingdoms of living things: plants and animals. Linnaeus published the final edition of this book in 1770. By that time, it was more than three thousand pages in three volumes.

INTRODUCING BINOMIAL NOMENCLATURE

After Linnaeus published the first edition of *System of Nature*, he spent much of his time collecting plants and organizing botanical gardens. He also kept writing about plants and classification. In 1740 Linnaeus's mentor, Olof Rudbeck, died. Linnaeus eagerly accepted Rudbeck's job at Uppsala University and continued working there for the rest of his career. Eventually he published more than one hundred books on botany and classification.

Linnaeus published one of his most important works in 1753. In *Plant Species*, he uses his classification system to organize more than eighteen thousand plant species. He also introduces a new method for naming each species.

LINNAEUS'S SYSTEM IN ACTION Linnaeus's system for organizing living things is the foundation of the classification system many modern scientists use. But over time, scientists have refined his system. Modern scientists recognize seven ranks instead of Linnaeus's six. The new rank is between kingdom and class. It's called a phylum in the animal kingdom. (The plural form of *phylum* is *phyla*.)

Many modern scientists divide the animal kingdom into about thirty-five phyla. For example, alligators belong to the chordate phylum. Each member of this group has a backbone. Each phylum consists of many classes. Alligators belong to the reptile class because they have scaly skin and lay eggs.

Scientists divide each class into orders. Alligators belong to the crocodilian order. Crocodilians are large, fierce meat eaters that live in warm, wet places. Scientists divide each order into families. All crocodilians belong to the crocodylidian family.

Scientists divide each family into genera. All the world's alligators belong to the *Alligator* genus. Each genus is made up of one or more species. Most modern scientists recognize two alligator species: *Alligator mississippiensis* and *Alligator sinensis.*

Classifying all of Earth's organisms is no easy task! The number of groups within each rank is always changing. As scientists study living things, they learn more and more about how organisms are—and aren't—related. As they learn, they often move organisms from one group to another. Sometimes they create brand-new groups or combine old ones.

For example, in 2007 DNA tests of bats in Guyana turned up some surprises. Researchers suggested creating six new bat species. As scientists continue to study organisms' DNA, they'll probably make even more changes to the tree of life.

During Linnaeus's time, scientific names for living things were long and complex. They might include up to fifteen Latin words. For example, the scientific name for the European honeybee was *Apis pubescens, thorace subgriseo, abdomine fusco, pedibus posticis glabris utrinque margine ciliatis.*

Even worse, no naming rules existed. If a naturalist didn't like a name, he could simply use a different name. For example, botanists disagreed about the best name for the common wild briar rose. Some called it *Rosa sylvestris inodora seu canina.* Others called it *Rosa sylvestris alba cum rubore, folio glabro.* The lack of naming rules made it hard for naturalists to discuss specific organisms.

Linnaeus wanted to end the confusion, so he developed a simpler naming system. He'd read Caspar Bauhin's work and liked the idea of two-word names. He saw that he could combine Bauhin's naming strategy with the genus and species concepts he'd already borrowed from Joseph Pitton de Tournefort and John Ray. The result would be scientific names that everyone could easily understand and remember.

Linnaeus called his new naming system binomial nomenclature. To come up with this term, he combined several Latin words. *Bi* means "two," and *nomen* means "name," so *binomial* means "two names." *Nomen* reappears in the first half of the word *nomenclature.* The second half of the word comes from *calator*, which means "caller" or "call out." So *nomenclature* means "calling by name." When scientists use binomial nomenclature, they are calling living things by two names.

Carl Linnaeus

The first word in a binomial scientific name is the organism's genus. The second word is the organism's species. We always italicize genus and species names to make them immediately recognizable as scientific names. We capitalize the first letter of the genus name and lowercase the first letter of the species name.

For example, *Quercus rubra* is the scientific name for the red oak tree. *Quercus alba* is the scientific name for the white oak tree. Because all oak trees are in the same genus, their scientific names all begin the same way. The genus name *Quercus* is the Latin word for "oak." The species name *rubra* is the Latin word for "red," and *alba* is the Latin word for "white."

Linnaeus first used his new naming system consistently when he wrote *Plant Species*. He incorporated these plant names and introduced two-word names for animals when he revised *System of Nature* in 1758. For example, he named the common wild briar rose *Rosa canina.* He named the European honeybee *Apis mellifera.*

What's in a Name?

When a scientist discovers a species, he or she has the honor of naming it. A newfound organism usually fits into an existing genus. For the species name, a scientist often chooses an adjective that describes an obvious trait, the location where the organism lives, or the person who discovered it.

Scientists are expected to follow certain naming rules, but new names don't need approval unless someone complains. The International Commission on Zoological Nomenclature handles any problems with animal names. Similar groups handle questions or concerns about the names of plants, fungi, and bacteria.

Linnaeus often named species after people he knew. He gave a small, useless weed the genus name *Siegesbeckia* after Johann Siegesbeck, a botanist who denounced Linnaeus's classification system. He named *Rudbeckia,* a genus of plants that includes black-eyed Susans, in honor of his mentor, Olof Rudbeck. Linnaeus named his favorite plant *Linnaea borealis* after himself. Modern scientists still use this scientific name to describe the twinflower, a small plant with delicate blue flowers.

Sometimes scientists show their sense of humor in naming newfound organisms. When paleontologists Scott Sampson and David Krause discovered a new dinosaur in Madagascar (formerly the Malagasy Republic) in 1999, they decided to call the ferocious predator *Masiakasaurus knopfleri. Masiakasaurus* is a Latin combination of the Malagasy word for "vicious" and the Greek word for "lizard." But the second part of the name honors Mark Knopfler, the lead singer of the rock band Dire Straits. The scientists say one of the band's songs was playing on the radio when they found the bones.

Madison High School Library
3498 Treat Rd
Adrian, MI 49221

Naturalists across Europe immediately saw the advantages of Linnaeus's new system. It quickly became the standard way of naming species. Scientists still use most of Linnaeus's binomial scientific names.

LINNAEUS'S LEGACY

Shortly after completing the 1770 edition of *System of Nature*, Linnaeus began to have health problems. He resigned from Uppsala University in 1777 and died in 1778.

At the end of his life, as Linnaeus looked back on his accomplishments, he wrote: "I have built anew the whole science of natural history from the ground up, to the point where it is today; I do not know whether anyone now can venture forward without being led by my hand."

This statement may seem arrogant, but it's completely true. Linnaeus had single-handedly developed a clever system for organizing both plants and animals. His system helped naturalists better understand the world around them. The new system became even more valuable as European explorers and naturalists traveled to the far corners of the world and brought back boatloads of newfound plants and animals. Scientists needed to study each newfound organism and give it a position on the tree of life. The Linnaean classification system seemed perfect for the job.

CHAPTER 3

CLASSIFICATION MEETS EVOLUTION

Most naturalists were completely satisfied with Carl Linnaeus's system for classifying animals, but not Jean-Baptiste Lamarck. In 1778, the same year Carl Linnaeus died, Lamarck became an assistant botanist at the Jardin des Plantes in Paris, France. When the institution was re-organized and renamed the Muséum National d'Histoire Naturelle in 1793, Lamarck was promoted to a new position: professor of insects and worms.

At the time, Lamarck knew nothing about insects or worms, but he learned quickly. Within a few years, he had invented the term *invertebrate* to describe all the creatures in the museum's large collection of creepy crawlies. Like many other scientific words, *invertebrate* is a combination of Latin terms. *In* means "not." *Vertebra* means "joint" and refers to the joints in the spine, or backbone. Thus invertebrates are animals without backbones.

Lamarck organized the museum's invertebrate collection and classified the animals in it. In the process, he created several new animal groups. These included mollusks, arachnids, crustaceans, annelids, and flatworms.

As Lamarck studied the museum's invertebrate fossils, he saw strong evidence that a species can change over time, or evolve. This was an unpopular idea. Most people believed that God had created every species on Earth exactly as it was. Lamarck wasn't the only naturalist thinking about evolution, but he was one of the first to state his ideas boldly in writing.

In 1809 Lamarck published *Zoological Philosophy*. In this book, he suggests that as a habitat changes, living things alter their behavior to survive. If the members of a species begin using a certain body part more, that part slowly grows bigger and stronger. If the members of a species use a body part less, that part slowly shrinks and weakens. It might even disappear.

Jean-Baptiste Lamarck

Lamarck also claims that an individual organism can pass body changes acquired during its lifetime to its offspring. As a result, says Lamarck, members of a species change continually as they adapt to their habitat.

To support his ideas, Lamarck points to the

giraffe's long neck. He claims that if a giraffe repeatedly stretched its neck to reach the highest branches of trees, the neck would gradually lengthen. He thought that when a long-necked giraffe had a youngster, the baby's neck would also be extra long because of its parent's stretching. This idea seems silly now. But during Lamarck's time, no one understood that traits pass from parent to offspring via genes (pieces of DNA). An organism's environment, activities, and experiences usually don't affect genes.

Many people ridiculed Lamarck. They just couldn't accept an idea that contradicted their religious beliefs. But Lamarck's thoughts on evolution greatly influenced later naturalists. One of them was Charles Darwin.

WHAT DARWIN DID FOR SCIENCE

In 1831, a few months after graduating from the University of Cambridge in Britain, twenty-two-year-old Charles Darwin joined the crew of the *Beagle*. As the ship's naturalist, Darwin was supposed to collect plants, animals, rocks, and fossils during the *Beagle*'s five-year voyage around the world. Darwin took his job seriously. He carefully observed the places he visited and made detailed notes about what he saw.

When the *Beagle* returned to Britain in 1836, Darwin had a large collection of specimens and notebooks full of information. He also had the seed of a theory that would change the way scientists thought about life on Earth. Darwin describes the development of his ideas on evolution in the first paragraph of his 1859 book *The Origin of*

Species: "When on board *H.M.S. Beagle* as Naturalist, I was much struck with certain facts in the distribution of the [creatures] inhabiting South America, and in the geological relations of the present to the past inhabitants of that continent. These facts . . . seemed to throw some light on the origin of species—that mystery of mysteries, as it has been called by one of our greatest philosophers."

Darwin spent many years thinking about what he'd seen on his voyage. He also read many books and thought about how the authors' ideas related to the theory he was slowly developing in his mind.

When he received a not-yet-published essay from fellow naturalist and world traveler Alfred Russel Wallace, Darwin rushed to set his ideas down clearly on paper. Wallace's essay included most of the ideas Darwin had been thinking about for years. Darwin knew that if he didn't hurry to publish his ideas, he'd receive no credit for his long hours of work.

Why is *The Origin of Species* such an important book? Many people think it's because in it Darwin introduces the theory of evolution, but they're wrong. Educated people all over Europe had been discussing and debating evolution for many years. *The Origin of Species* is famous for presenting the theory of natural selection—the method by which evolution occurs.

According to Darwin, no two organisms are identical. Each individual has unique inborn traits that are slightly different from those of other members of its species. Some traits improve an organism's ability to survive in its habitat. Others make survival more difficult. Still others have no effect on an organism's ability to survive. These differing inborn traits, or variations, pass from parent to offspring. An organism that inherits a positive variation—an adaptation that helps it survive—has an advantage over fellow species members living in the same habitat.

For example, a bird with an inborn trait that helps it find food more easily or defend itself against enemies better can spend more time reproducing and caring for its young. All its offspring have the same adaptation and the same advantage. Over time, the members of this bird species that have the positive variation thrive. Those without it die off (go extinct). In this way, all species on Earth change over time.

Darwin explains in *The Origin of Species*, "It may be said that natural selection is daily and hourly scrutinizing, throughout the world, every variation, even the slightest; rejecting that which is bad, preserving and adding up all that is good; silently and insensibly working, whenever and wherever opportunity offers, at the improvement of each [species] in relation to its [environment]. We see nothing of these slow changes in progress,

Charles Darwin

until the hand of time has marked the long lapses of ages, and then . . . we only see that the forms of life are now different from what they formerly were."

Why did Darwin take his time thinking about how to write *The Origin of Species*? Because evolution was a controversial topic. He knew he had to include solid evidence to back up his ideas, and finding supporting examples was time consuming. As he discusses each point, he gives examples from his wide knowledge of barnacles, bees, snakes, finches, and other animals. He describes where and suggests why evolution has occurred in specific organisms.

Darwin's publication of *The Origin of Species* gained him many loyal supporters as well as many harsh critics. People spent hours on end debating evolution and natural selection, but Darwin avoided the controversy. He spent most of his time revising and expanding his book until he published the final edition in 1872.

DARWIN'S IDEAS ABOUT CLASSIFICATION

During his later years, Darwin became more interested in taxonomy. By this time, Europeans had been using Linnaeus's classification system for more than a century. But Darwin thought the system had some serious flaws. He didn't like Linnaeus's criteria for classifying plants.

You may recall that Linnaeus sorted plants into classes based on the number and position of the flowers' stamens. He divided classes into orders based on the appearance of the flowers' pistils (female reproductive organs).

Why did Linnaeus think reproductive organs made good criteria for classification? In 1694 a German botanist named Rudolf Jakob Camerer had discovered how flowering plants reproduce. Throughout the 1700s, botanists marveled at the similarities between plant and animal reproduction. The popular fascination with pistils and stamens made them obvious choices for Linnaeus's taxonomic criteria.

Also, in the 1700s, most people believed that God had created every species exactly as it was. They had no inkling that species evolve to survive better in their habitats. As a result, they didn't understand that some organisms are more closely related than others. When Linnaeus classified plants and animals, he used criteria that made sense to him. But he wasn't trying to show evolutionary relationships. He didn't know those relationships existed.

By Darwin's time, people were no longer so fascinated with plant reproduction. Many naturalists had serious doubts about using pistils and stamens as classification criteria. They thought some of Linnaeus's plant groupings were arbitrary and unnatural. For example, a few flowering plants ended up in the same order as pines, firs, and other trees that use cones to reproduce. By the mid-1800s, most naturalists agreed that cone-bearing trees and flowering plants were so different that they belonged in separate classes. (Modern scientists classify them in separate phyla.)

Darwin called for a more natural system of plant classification. He thought classification should do more than sort organisms into arbitrary groups. He urged scientists to choose criteria that showed evolutionary relationships.

Darwin believed that the more traits two organisms share, the more closely related they probably are. According to Darwin, pines and firs belong in the same group because they have many traits in common. They both grow as trees. They both have needlelike leaves. And they both reproduce using cones. All these similarities suggest that pines and firs are closely related.

Although Darwin disapproved of Linnaeus's plant classification criteria, he thought Linnaeus's criteria for classifying animals made more sense. For example, Linnaeus grouped orangutans, chimpanzees, and humans together in the hominid family. He placed hominids, lemurs, and monkeys together in the primate order. These groupings seemed more natural and logical to Darwin, and they've held up well over time. Scientists still use them.

Why was Linnaeus so much more successful at classifying related animals? Because he grouped them according to a wider variety of similar traits. And the combinations of traits Linnaeus chose tended to reflect evolutionary relationships.

Not everyone agreed with Darwin's insistence that classification should reflect evolution. Many people were reluctant to abandon or modify a system naturalists had been using for more than one hundred years. In fact, it took another century for scientists to come around to Darwin's way of thinking. And modern researchers still disagree about the best way to combine evolutionary evidence with anatomical and behavioral information.

CHAPTER 4

ADDING NEW KINGDOMS

One of Charles Darwin's biggest supporters was a German biologist named Ernst Haeckel. Haeckel had just graduated from medical school when *The Origin of Species* came out. He traveled all over Europe and lectured enthusiastically on evolution by natural selection. Later, Haeckel became interested in single-celled organisms. He spent many hours studying them under a microscope.

A THIRD KINGDOM: PROTISTS

Even though microscopes had been around since the 1600s, Earth's tiniest organisms hadn't received much attention until the 1800s. In 1845 a German scientist named Karl Theodor Ernst von Siebold had published the first book about a group of single-celled organisms he called protozoa. Despite their tiny size, Siebold's protozoa could move around on their own and hunt for food. No one had ever classified these microorganisms, so Siebold suggested adding protozoa to the animal kingdom.

Louis Agassiz, a Swiss doctor and naturalist, disagreed with Siebold's proposal. He thought protozoa had more in common with protophyta, which were in the plant kingdom, than with animals. Protophyta are single-celled organisms. Like plants, they use photosynthesis to make their own food. Inside a plant's body, sunlight powers a series of chemical reactions. These reactions change water and carbon dioxide into oxygen, which plants release into the air, and a sugar called glucose. Glucose gives plants all the energy they need to live and grow.

Ernst Haeckel

In 1866 Haeckel decided to lump all single-celled organisms into one group called protists. He didn't think protists should be classified as plants or animals. According to Haeckel, protists were so unique and unusual that they deserved their own kingdom. It was the first time someone had suggested a major change to Linnaeus's classification system. But it wouldn't be the last.

A FOURTH KINGDOM: BACTERIA

Haeckel's protist kingdom included a group of very small, very simple single-celled organisms that modern scientists call bacteria. Haeckel was curious about these tiny organisms, but he didn't realize just how special they are. No one did until the 1930s, when a French marine biologist named Edouard Chatton studied bacteria with the best microscopes available.

As Chatton examined the internal structures of a wide variety of bacteria, he realized how truly different they are from all other living things. He proposed dividing life on Earth into two groups: the prokaryotes (before nucleus) and the eukaryotes (true nucleus). The prokaryote group includes all bacteria. A prokaryote is a tiny, single-celled organism with no nucleus (a large, central compartment in some cells that contains DNA) and only one

Prokaryotic Cell Structure

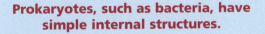

DNA

Prokaryotes, such as bacteria, have simple internal structures.

kind of organelle (internal structure). A prokaryote's DNA floats freely in the cell, and it reproduces by splitting in half. The eukaryote group consists of plants, animals, fungi, and protists. Eukaryotes are larger and more complex than prokaryotes. Some are single-celled. Others contain many cells. A typical eukaryotic cell has several different kinds of organelles and a nucleus that contains DNA. Eukaryotes reproduce in a much more complicated way than prokaryotes do.

When American biologist Herbert Copeland heard about Chatton's discovery, he thought that bacteria

Eukaryotic Cell Structure

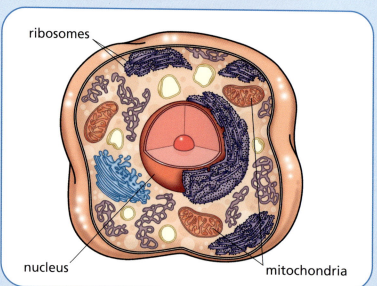

ribosomes

nucleus

mitochondria

Eukaryotes contain a number of organelles, or internal structures, such as a nucleus, ribosomes (small dots), and mitochondria.

deserved their own kingdom. In 1938 he wrote a paper proposing this idea. Other scientists immediately saw the advantages of Copeland's four-kingdom system.

Copeland later wrote two more papers that more clearly defined which creatures belonged in each of his four kingdoms. He eventually developed the term *protoctist* to describe a kingdom that included Haeckel's single-celled protists (minus the bacteria) as well as some simple multicellular organisms previously classified in the plant kingdom.

A FIFTH KINGDOM: FUNGI

In the 1950s, an American ecologist named Robert Whittaker questioned Copeland's four-kingdom classification system. Copeland, like Linnaeus and Haeckel, had included fungi in the plant kingdom. But as Whittaker studied forest ecosystems (how forests function overall), he realized that plants and fungi play very different roles.

Plants are producers. They use photosynthesis to make their own food. Fungi, such as mushrooms, yeasts, molds, and puffballs, get energy in a very different way. They're decomposers, nature's recyclers.

Most fungi live in the soil and feed on dead plants and animals. Fungi release digestive enzymes from their bodies. The enzymes break down food particles so the fungi can absorb nutrients into their cells. These nutrients give fungi the energy they need to live and grow. If a fungus doesn't use any of the nutrients it has broken down, nearby plants can take up those nutrients by their roots.

In this way, fungi continuously recycle important nutrients through an ecosystem.

Because fungi aren't photosynthesizers, Whittaker thought they didn't belong in the plant kingdom. In 1957 he suggested a new four-kingdom classification system that differed from Copeland's. Whittaker's system consisted of a plant kingdom, an animal kingdom, a protist kingdom, and a fungi kingdom. At the time, he wasn't convinced that bacteria were different enough from other single-celled organisms to warrant their own kingdom. But after reading papers published by Canadian microbiologist Roger Stanier in 1962 and 1964, Whittaker changed his mind. In 1969 he revised his classification system to include a fifth kingdom for bacteria.

Bacteria come in many different shapes, such as rod-shaped *Bacillus subtilis (left)* and spiral-shaped *Streptomyces virginiae (right).*

By this time, Whittaker was a well-known and respected scientist. His five-kingdom system intrigued researchers all over the world. Lynn Margulis, a young microbiologist at Boston University, was particularly impressed.

In 1970 Margulis published her own version of the tree of life. It featured Whittaker's fungi kingdom, but her protist kingdom was a bit different. It included algae, a diverse group that contains seaweed and some other photosynthesizers. Whittaker had classified algae as plants. But Margulis's studies showed that algae have more in common with protists than they do with plants.

Margulis and her colleague, Karlene Schwartz, would eventually make more changes to Whittaker's five-kingdom system. But before that could happen, the field of classification had to turn upside down and inside out.

CHAPTER 5

THE BIRTH OF CLADISTICS

By the mid-1900s, scientists around the world accepted Charles Darwin's theory of evolution by natural selection. But they still used physical features to classify living things. Even though many scientists agreed that a classification system based on evolutionary relationships would be useful, they couldn't see a way to put such a system into practice. Why not? Because sometimes it's very hard to determine which organisms are most closely related. Shared traits suggest a recent common ancestor (and thus a close relationship), but they don't guarantee it. Two organisms may have similar traits inherited from different ancestors.

For example, birds, bees, and bats all have wings. But their wings are built differently. Their ancestors' fossils show that wings developed three separate times in three different ways. Birds, bees, and bats didn't inherit their wings from a common ancestor. So they aren't closely related.

The animals' similar trait, wings, is the result of convergent evolution. To *converge* means "to come together" or "to merge." According to the theory of convergent evolution, very different groups of organisms living in similar environments gradually evolve body features that look similar and function in similar ways. The common feature helps all the animals survive in their environments. Wings, for example, help birds, bees, and bats escape from predators and move across large areas of land quickly.

SHOWING EVOLUTIONARY RELATIONSHIPS

Willi Hennig understood the problem of convergent evolution, but he felt very strongly that evolutionary relationships should be used to bring order to the natural world. In the late 1940s, Hennig, a German scientist, began developing a completely new system for showing relationships among Earth's vast array of living things. The result of his work was a landmark paper published in 1950. It proposed an idea that modern scientists call cladistics.

The goal of cladistics is to show evolutionary relationships among organisms by focusing on derived characters. A derived character is a trait inherited from a common ancestor. If two organisms share a derived character, they must also share the gene responsible for that trait. The more of these sections of DNA two organisms share, the more closely they're related.

Humans and chimpanzees share many derived characters. And in fact, scientists discovered in 2005 that more than 98 percent of our DNA is the same. This means we're very closely related to chimps. Our common ancestor lived about five million years ago. You share even more derived characters with your brother or sister. Your genes are almost exactly the same because you have two common—and very recent—ancestors, your parents.

Among the many species of birds, a key derived character is feathers. All birds have feathers, but no other animals do. That's because only birds have the DNA that makes feathers form. All birds inherited this DNA from a common ancestor that lived about 150 million years ago. After that time, different bird populations went through many different changes. Swans and geese developed webbed feet to help them swim. Parrots developed brightly colored plumage to help them survive in tropical rain forests. Chickadees and blue jays developed beaks perfectly suited for cracking open seeds. But because all these bird species share a unique derived character—feathers—scientists group them together in the same class.

Swans are more distantly related to iguanas than they are to geese, parrots, chickadees, and blue jays. An iguana is a reptile, not a bird. Its body is covered with scales instead of feathers. But if you go back far enough in time (about 300 million years), swans and iguanas do have a common ancestor. How do scientists know this? Because swans and iguanas share a derived character: two holes in their skull between the nostrils and the eyes. All birds and all reptiles have these holes, but no other animals do. The holes show that swans are more closely related to iguanas than they are to porcupines, jellyfish, or butterflies.

Even though Hennig first described cladistics in 1950, most scientists didn't hear about it until 1966. That's when scholars translated Hennig's paper into English. But even then, his idea didn't catch on right away.

The key to cladistics is identifying shared derived characters. But in the late 1960s, scientists weren't sure how to recognize derived characters in organisms—especially lesser-known ones. Luckily the solution to that problem was just a few years away. It came from scientists studying the internal workings of cells.

WHAT'S A CLADOGRAM?

A cladogram is a branched, treelike diagram that scientists use to show evolutionary relationships among species. These relationships are based on shared derived characters—features that different species inherited from a common ancestor. By looking at a cladogram, it's easy to see which organisms in the diagram are more closely related and which are more distantly related. If you follow any two branches of the cladogram back to the point where they intersect, you can get a general idea of how long ago the common ancestor of two organisms lived. Sometimes a cladogram includes a time scale. With a time scale, you can determine more precisely how long ago the common ancestor lived.

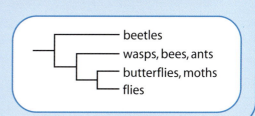

beetles
wasps, bees, ants
butterflies, moths
flies

INSIDE THE CELL

Cells are the basic units of all organisms. Cells are the smallest structures that can perform all the chemical processes necessary for life, from turning food into energy to reproducing. Bacteria and some protists consist of just one cell, but all other organisms contain many cells. Your body contains about one hundred trillion cells. They're grouped into tissues, organs, and organ systems. These cell groups all work together to help you live and grow.

The most important molecule inside a cell is DNA. Segments of DNA contain the instructions a cell needs to build hundreds or thousands of different proteins. Each protein is a long string of molecules called amino acids. The order of amino acids determines what task a protein will perform. For example, structural proteins build or repair parts of the cell. Proteins called enzymes make chemical reactions occur more quickly or at lower temperatures. Without proteins, cells couldn't function.

By the early 1950s, scientists knew that DNA's basic chemical components are phosphate, a sugar called deoxyribose, and four different nucleotide bases: adenine (A), cytosine (C), guanine (G), and thymine (T). Scientists also knew that C always bonds with G and that A always bonds with T. But no one knew how the rest of DNA's components fit together.

In 1952 a British chemist named Rosalind Franklin used X-rays to create some excellent pictures of DNA. When American biologist James Watson and British biophysicist Francis Crick saw those images, they understood DNA's basic shape. It's a double helix, a structure that looks like a twisted ladder. The sides of the ladder consist of repeating sugar-phosphate units. They support the ladder's rungs, which are bonded pairs of nucleotide bases.

James Watson *(left)* and Francis Crick *(right)* created a model of the double helix structure of a DNA molecule.

MAKING CLADISTICS PRACTICAL

After scientists finally understood DNA's structure, they could move on to the next question: how does DNA direct protein production? During the 1960s, researchers worked hard to understand this process, which they called translation. They eventually realized that translation is almost exactly the same in all living things. That meant translation had developed in a common ancestor that lived billions of years ago.

In about 1970, an American scientist named Carl Woese began to wonder exactly how translation had developed and how it had evolved over time. But before Woese could study

DNA Decoded

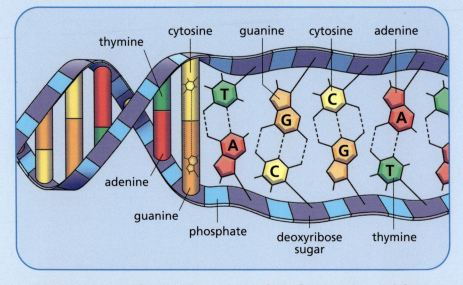

DNA consists of repeating sugar-phosphate units and four nucleotide bases: adenine, thymine, cytosine, and guanine. The bases bond in pairs. Adenine always bonds with thymine, and cytosine always bonds with guanine.

the evolution of translation, he needed to know how all living things are related to one another. No one had that information. And Woese knew it wouldn't be easy to figure out.

Most scientists were still classifying plants and animals by comparing their physical features. Woese knew that approach wouldn't work for bacteria. Because bacteria are so small and because scientists hadn't studied them as much as bigger organisms, scientists knew little about their physical traits. And they certainly didn't know which shared traits suggest evolutionary relationships.

Molecular biology, a brand-new branch of science, came to his rescue. Molecular biology is the study of molecules found in living things. A few molecular biologists were discovering the advantages of using cellular molecules such as proteins to understand evolutionary relationships.

Like physical traits, molecular traits pass from one generation to the next. But because most cellular molecules aren't in direct contact with an organism's environment, they aren't affected by convergent evolution. As a result, molecular traits are often much more reliable indicators of evolutionary relationships. Distantly related organisms sometimes have similar physical traits, but they never have similar molecular traits.

For example, sharks and dolphins both have fins. If scientists use physical traits as classification criteria, they might assume these two ocean animals are closely related. But if scientists study the molecules inside the cells of these animals, they see some big differences. Even though sharks and dolphins have similar body parts, they're not closely related. Their common ancestor lived about four hundred million years ago.

If scientists then compare the molecular traits of dolphins and whales, they see a lot of similarities. That's because the common ancestor of dolphins and whales, both marine mammals, lived less than forty million years ago. So while a quick look suggests that dolphins are more closely related to sharks than to whales, the molecules inside their cells reveal the true evolutionary story.

Before long, Woese realized that he could combine cladistics with the latest molecular biology techniques to understand how different bacteria species are related to one another. And by comparing bacterial molecules to similar molecules in other living things, he could slowly build a universal evolutionary tree.

In the early 1970s, most of the molecular biologists interested in understanding evolutionary relationships were focusing on proteins. They thought that if the order of amino acids in a specific protein was exactly the same in two creatures, those creatures must be very closely related. If there were a few differences in the sequence of amino acids, the organisms were not as closely related. The more differences in the amino acid sequence, the more distantly the creatures were related.

But Woese discovered that it was easier to work with ribosomal ribonucleic acid (rRNA). RNA molecules are similar to DNA molecules in many ways, but there are two key differences. First, RNA has just one sugar-phosphate strand instead of two. Second, RNA's four nucleotide bases are cytosine, guanine, adenine, and uracil (instead of DNA's thymine).

The cells of living things contain several different kinds of RNA. Each one plays a specific role in protein production. A cell's ribosomes, the tiny structures that assemble proteins during translation, contain rRNA. The rRNA helps string amino acids together into proteins.

For most of the mid-1970s, Woese compared the sequence of nucleotides in rRNA samples from hundreds of different bacteria species. When he found two bacteria species with very similar rRNA sequences, he knew they must be very closely related. Their common ancestor lived more recently than the common ancestor of bacteria species with very different rRNA sequences.

CHAPTER 6

KINGDOMS OR DOMAINS?

When a German microbiologist named Ralph Wolfe heard what Carl Woese was doing, he contacted Woese. He suggested that Woese study the rRNA of some unusual bacteria. These oddballs somehow survive in the world's most extreme environments. Some live in boiling water or supersalty ponds. Others live inside volcanoes or buried deep in the Antarctic ice.

A SIXTH KINGDOM: ARCHAEA

As Woese and Wolfe compared the rRNA sequences of the typical bacteria and the oddballs, they noticed some big differences. In fact, the oddballs had as much in common with plants and animals as they did with typical bacteria. Woese was stunned.

To emphasize the importance of his discovery, Woese divided bacteria into two groups. Modern scientists call the typical bacteria eubacteria, or simply bacteria, and they call the oddballs archaea. Woese believed that archaea were so different from all other living things that they deserved their own kingdom. In 1977 he wrote a paper that proposed a six-kingdom classification system.

RESTRUCTURING THE TREE OF LIFE

In 1990 Woese made an even more startling announcement. He wanted to replace his six-kingdom, Linnaean classification system with a new one. With Woese's new system, scientists would never group organisms according to physical or behavioral similarities. Instead, they would use only data from studying the sequences of rRNA and other molecules.

The evolutionary tree Woese created from studying rRNA sequences was full of surprises. His research showed that plants, animals, fungi, and protists have more in common with one another than archaea have in common with eubacteria. As a result, Woese proposed dividing life on Earth into three separate domains: archaea, eubacteria, and eukarya (plants, animals, fungi, and protists).

Each of Woese's domains contained subgroups called divisions. Animals, plants, and fungi are all separate divisions within the eukarya domain. So are many of Robert Whittaker's protist phyla. Woese's classification system emphasizes microorganisms much more than other systems do. It's a whole new way of thinking about life on Earth.

Some scientists immediately accepted Woese's three-domain system. But many remained skeptical. Some critics thought Woese's system overemphasized microorganisms. Others felt Woese's rRNA studies didn't provide

Woese's Three Domains

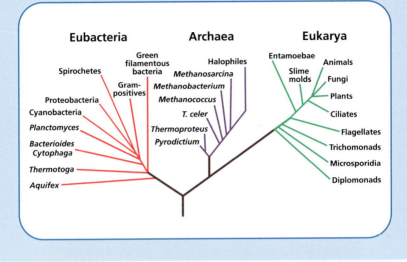

enough evidence to classify microorganisms with certainty. They wanted to see other kinds of evidence supporting Woese's system.

But no other evidence existed. Microscopes could provide information about the sizes and shapes of microorganisms and their internal structures, but that wasn't enough to determine evolutionary relationships. According to Roger Stanier, "It was as if you went to a zoo and had no way of telling the lions from the elephants from the orangutans—or any of these from the trees."

TWO NEW TOOLS

By the mid-1990s, molecular biologists were using two powerful new tools. The first was a new generation of computers with large memories that could process data faster than ever. The second was a technique called polymerase chain reaction (PCR). Kary Mullis, an American chemist, had developed PCR in 1983. It allowed scientists to copy DNA pieces quickly and efficiently. Using these new tools, scientists could easily work out the order of nucleotides in any organism's DNA. As a result, scientists could compare DNA from many different organisms.

In 1996 a team of scientists led by Carol Bult of the Institute for Genomic Research in Rockville, Maryland, successfully sequenced the entire genome (all the genetic

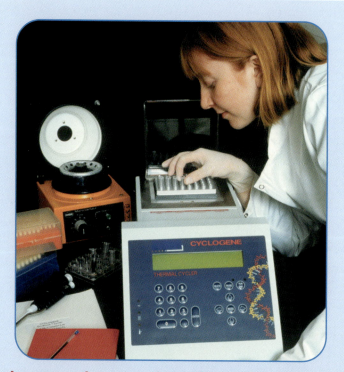

A virus researcher uses a heat plate to clone DNA fragments during a polymerase chain reaction.

material) of an archaea. The scientists found that some of the archaea's genes resembled those of eubacteria. Other archaea genes had more in common with eukarya genes. These findings matched Woese's rRNA research results and supported his three-domain classification system.

SWAPPING AND STEALING DNA

By the summer of 1998, scientists had sequenced the genomes of more than a dozen prokaryotes. As researchers studied and compared these microorganisms' DNA, they found that some eubacteria contained genes like the ones found in archaea. The researchers had expected this because they knew Woese's and Bult's work. But they also found a big surprise: some eubacteria had genes that closely resembled those of eukarya. What was going on? Eubacteria were supposed to be completely different from eukarya.

Eventually scientists realized that these findings supported a theory Lynn Margulis had proposed in 1967. According to Margulis, all eukarya evolved from prokaryotes. Where was her evidence? Inside cells.

As you may recall, all eukarya cells contain a variety of tiny, independent structures called organelles. Each organelle performs a specific task that helps the cell function. For example, ribosomes help build proteins, and mitochondria break down food and supply other parts of the cell with energy. Most kinds of organelles are found in all eukarya, but chloroplasts aren't. Only plants and other photosynthesizers have chloroplasts. Chloroplasts absorb energy from sunlight and use this energy to power photosynthesis.

As Margulis studied mitochondria and chloroplasts, she discovered that these organelles have their own DNA. At first, Margulis couldn't imagine why. But then she had an idea. Maybe these organelles had once been independent organisms. Margulis suggested that at some point in Earth's history, prokaryotes fused to form the world's first eukarya. Some of the prokaryotes' DNA became part of the new eukaryotic cell's genome. The rest of the DNA remained in the organelles.

Margulis also realized that some bacteria steal genes from the microorganisms they eat. Other bacteria swap genes as casually as ten-year-olds trade baseball cards. This stealing and swapping has been going on for billions of years. As a result, bacterial genomes are often a hodgepodge of genes from many different sources. This means that two microorganisms with similar genes could be as closely related as humans and chimpanzees or as distantly related as toads and tulips.

What's the upshot of all this? Genome sequencing gives scientists a wealth of knowledge about bacteria, but it can't be used to classify them.

ANIMAL RELATIONS

Even though we can't compare DNA sequences to figure out evolutionary relationships among bacteria, we can use DNA to classify plants and animals. DNA comparison usually confirms classification decisions based on physical and behavioral similarities among plants and animals. But there have been a few surprises.

For example, scientists used to classify skunks in the

same family as badgers, ferrets, and minks. But DNA comparisons in the mid-1990s showed that skunks aren't closely related to these other animals. Modern scientists classify skunks in a family all their own.

DNA studies also resolved a long-standing debate about how to classify the giant panda. A giant panda looks a lot like a bear, but it doesn't eat like one. Most bears eat a lot of meat. Polar bears, for example, eat a steady diet of fish and seal meat. Other bear species eat meat (such as fish and dead animals) and other foods (such as berries). A giant panda eats bamboo (a kind of grass) almost all the time.

Some scientists believed that the giant panda is more closely related to the red panda than it is to bears. The red panda is a smaller bamboo-eating animal that lives in the same Asian forests as giant pandas. Red pandas look like raccoons with rusty red fur.

In 1995 scientists compared DNA from giant pandas, several bear species, red pandas, and raccoons. The comparison showed that giant pandas are most closely related to bears. Modern scientists classify giant pandas as members of the bear family.

CHOOSING A CLASSIFICATION SYSTEM

Even though DNA sequencing didn't produce solid evidence for Woese's three-domain system, many modern scientists do use Woese's system to classify living things. The other popular system is an updated version of Linnaeus's system Margulis and her colleague Karlene Schwartz developed.

Five-Kingdom Tree of Life

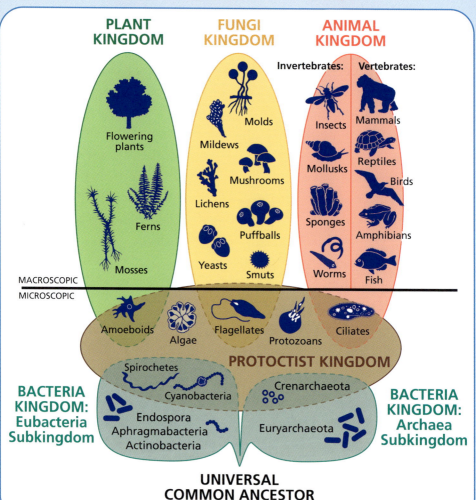

PLANT KINGDOM

Flowering plants
Ferns
Mosses

FUNGI KINGDOM

Molds
Mildews
Mushrooms
Lichens
Puffballs
Yeasts
Smuts

ANIMAL KINGDOM

Invertebrates:
Insects
Mollusks
Sponges
Worms

Vertebrates:
Mammals
Reptiles
Birds
Amphibians
Fish

MACROSCOPIC
MICROSCOPIC

Amoeboids
Algae
Flagellates
Protozoans
Ciliates

PROTOCTIST KINGDOM

Spirochetes
Cyanobacteria
Crenarchaeota

BACTERIA KINGDOM: Eubacteria Subkingdom

Endospora
Aphragmabacteria
Actinobacteria
Euryarchaeota

BACTERIA KINGDOM: Archaea Subkingdom

UNIVERSAL COMMON ANCESTOR

Lynn Margulis and Karlene Schwartz developed this five-kingdom classification system. In 1998 they revised the system, splitting the bacteria kingdom into two different subkingdoms, eubacteria and archaea.

In 1982 Margulis and Schwartz published *Five Kingdoms: An Illustrated Guide to the Phyla of Life on Earth*. By this time, Margulis was using Copeland's term *protoctist* and including a variety of multicellular organisms in that kingdom. But she and Schwartz rejected Woese's idea that archaea deserved a separate kingdom.

Margulis and Schwartz updated their book in 1988 and again in 1998. In the 1998 edition, they divide the bacteria kingdom into two subkingdoms: eubacteria and archaea. This change shows that Margulis and Schwartz recognize the value of Woese's work. But they still believe that the three-domain system overemphasizes a single line of evidence, rRNA sequences. Margulis and Schwartz prefer a classification system based on all available data, including information on physical traits, internal structures, and behavioral patterns as well as information from molecular studies.

So for modern scientists, two distinct classification systems exist side by side. Some people support Woese's three-domain system, while others prefer the more traditional, Linnaean, five-kingdom system. Still others try to blend the two systems. They use Woese's three domains but recognize four kingdoms (not fifteen divisions) within the eukarya domain.

THE BARCODE OF LIFE

Around the time Margulis and Schwartz published the 1998 edition of *Five Kingdoms*, an idea flashed through a Canadian researcher's mind. Paul Hebert of the University of Guelph wondered if scientists could build a handheld device with the power to quickly identify living things anytime, anywhere by analyzing their DNA.

Hebert called his idea DNA barcoding. DNA nucleotide sequences, like the Universal Product Codes (UPCs) on packaged products at the grocery store, are readable by high-tech scanning systems. A UPC is a series of bars that represents an eleven-digit number. The number identifies a product as peanut butter or cheese slices or cranberry juice. It also tells the store's cash registers the price of the product. An eleven-digit code allows one hundred billion unique numbers. So one hundred billion different products can have unique UPCs.

The DNA barcodes Hebert had in mind would identify species instead of products. When a scientist wanted to identify an organism, he or she would get a small sample from the organism's body, such as a bird's feather, a fish's scale, or a mammal's hair. Then the scientist would scan the first 650 nucleotide bases of a certain gene in the organism's DNA. A computer would compare the sequence of letters (As, Ts, Cs, and Gs) representing the nucleotides in the sample to all the nucleotide sequences stored in a gigantic database of known species. If the computer found a match, it would tell the scientist the organism's identity. If the computer didn't find a match, the scientist would know he or she had discovered an unknown species.

For DNA barcoding to work, Hebert had to find a gene that's nearly identical in all members of one species. The gene must also be markedly different in members of different species. After years of trial and error, Hebert settled on a gene called cytochrome c oxidase I (COI). Located in the mitochondrial DNA of every animal on Earth, COI contains the instructions to build a protein called cytochrome c. This protein helps cells use oxygen to generate energy.

In 2002 a small group of scientists began to take Hebert's idea seriously. After a series of meetings in 2003, the researchers formed the Consortium for the Barcode of Life (CBOL) in 2004. CBOL maintains the international DNA barcode database and coordinates DNA barcoding research projects all over the world.

So far, COI has been a perfect choice for barcoding fish, birds, insects, and mammals. But it doesn't work for all living things. Scientists can't use COI nucleotide sequences to identify amphibian species. It's not a good choice for identifying plants, protoctists, or prokaryotes either. Before we can use DNA barcoding to identify these organisms, scientists must find suitable genes to analyze. Botanists are testing possible genes in chloroplasts, but no one really knows when DNA barcoding will work for plants—or for other organisms outside the animal kingdom.

Despite this challenge, many scientists are excited about DNA barcoding. Since Linnaeus's time, people have identified about 1.7 million species. At that rate, it would take another 1,500 years to identify the 10 million or so eukarya species that scientists estimate live on Earth. DNA barcoding could do the job in a fraction of that time. Speed is important because scientists are in a hurry to catalog the diversity of life on

Earth. They want to complete the project before many of the creatures currently alive go extinct. DNA barcoding could also stop the illegal trade of exotic animals and help organize museum collections around the world.

But not everyone is enthusiastic about DNA barcoding. Some taxonomists worry that DNA barcodes won't always be able to tell apart closely related species. These scientists believe it's critical to use many different criteria when classifying a creature. They prefer a more traditional approach, which includes examining physical appearance, internal body structures, and behaviors as well as analyzing DNA.

According to Hebert and his colleagues, they don't intend DNA barcoding to replace other taxonomic techniques. Instead, they hope this new method will enhance traditional techniques by giving taxonomists a useful new tool.

Regardless of whether DNA barcoding turns out to be as valuable as it promises, scientists will continue to study Earth's incredible cast of creatures. As researchers examine living things, they'll make discoveries that allow more accurate classification than ever. But because life is so diverse and evolution is so complex, it will undoubtedly take many years for scientists to fully understand the tree of life.

DNA BARCODES AT WORK   DNA barcoding has proven very useful for some scientists. In 2004 scientists working in Costa Rica found that butterflies in the *Astraptes fulgerator* species had ten different barcodes. That meant the insects were really members of ten separate species.

Some researchers weren't surprised. They knew that even though all the adults in this group look similar, their caterpillars are quite different. The researchers had long suspected that the butterflies were of different species and that the adults' physical similarities must somehow protect them from predators. DNA barcoding gave these scientists the proof they needed.

In 2007 scientists barcoded 2,500 specimens of North American birds. They expected to detect 643 separate species, but they found some surprises. What scientists thought were 8 separate species of gulls turned out to be just 1. And in fifteen cases, birds that scientists had grouped in 1 species really belonged to 2 or more species.

Scientists studying bats in 2007 had similar results. When they barcoded 840 specimens that had come from Guyana, they detected all of the eighty species scientists had previously described. But they also found evidence that a few of the bat specimens classified in the same species are different enough that they should be considered separate species.

Glossary

adaptation: a feature that helps a living thing survive better in its environment

amino acids: the chemical compounds that make up proteins

archaea: a group of creatures that some scientists classify as bacteria but that have many traits in common with eukarya

bacteria: tiny, one-celled organisms that lack nuclei

binomial nomenclature: a system for naming organisms using two-word names, in which the first word is the genus name and the second word is the species name

chloroplast: a cellular organelle in plants and other photosynthesizers. It captures energy from sunlight and uses this energy to power photosynthesis.

cladistics: a system of classification based on the evolutionary relationships among organisms

cladogram: a branched diagram that shows evolutionary relationships among organisms

convergent evolution: when two or more distantly related groups of organisms develop a similar physical feature, usually because they live in the same environment. The common feature helps them survive in that environment.

derived character: in cladistics, traits inherited from a common ancestor

DNA (deoxyribonucleic acid): the molecule in every organism that contains genetic information. DNA passes from parent to offspring during reproduction.

eubacteria: the term used to describe all bacteria except archaea

eukaryote (eukarya): an organism whose cells have nuclei. Plants, animals, fungi, and protoctists are all eukaryotes.

evolve: to change over time

gene: a section of DNA that is associated with a particular trait

genome: all the genetic material in the chromosomes (structures made of DNA and proteins) of an organism

genus: a group of creatures within a family that share certain characteristics. A genus contains one or more species.

inherit: to receive genetic information from ancestors

mitochondria: cellular organelles that break down food molecules and make energy for the cell

molecular biology: the study of molecules in living things

nucleotide: one of the building blocks of DNA and RNA. Nucleotide bases (adenine, cytosine, guanine, and thymine or uracil) carry the instructions cells use to assemble proteins.

nucleus: the part of a eukaryotic cell that contains DNA

organelle: a tiny, independent structure within a cell. Each organelle carries out a specific task that helps the cell function.

prokaryote: a single-celled creature that lacks a nucleus

protein: a molecule made up of amino acids strung together based on directions from DNA. Structural proteins build or repair parts of the cell. Proteins called enzymes make chemical reactions occur more quickly or at a lower temperature.

protoctist (protist): a eukaryote that can't be classified as a plant, animal, or fungus. This group includes seaweeds, slime molds, and many other organisms.

ribosome: a cellular organelle that provides a surface for protein production

rRNA (ribosomal ribonucleic acid): a molecule in the ribosome that helps build proteins

species: a group of organisms within a genus that share certain characteristics. Members of a species can mate and produce healthy offspring.

taxonomy: the science of describing, identifying, naming, and classifying living things

translation: the process by which cells make proteins on the ribosomes

TIMELINE

CA. 350 B.C. Greek philosopher Aristotle develops his "ladder of nature" and begins classifying living things.

1544 William Turner publishes the first printed book devoted entirely to naming and describing birds.

1555 Pierre Belon suggests a system for classifying birds based on their body structures and habitats.

1583 Andrea Cesalpino describes fifteen hundred species of plants and suggests using their fruits, seeds, and other structures to classify them.

1596 Caspar Bauhin describes and classifies nearly six thousand plants and suggests using two-word scientific names to describe living things.

1682 John Ray describes more than eighteen thousand plant species using Latin scientific names and a classification system that emphasizes studying an organism as a whole.

1694 Joseph Pitton de Tournefort's *Elements of Botany* classifies more than ten thousand plant species and introduces the term *genus*.

1735 Carl Linnaeus publishes the first edition of *System of Nature*. He revises the book twelve times, publishing the final edition in 1770.

1753 Carl Linnaeus's *Plant Species* classifies more than eighteen thousand plants and introduces binomial nomenclature.

1809 Jean-Baptiste Lamarck presents his ideas about evolution in *Zoological Philosophy*.

1831–1836 Charles Darwin sails around the world aboard the *Beagle*.

1845 Karl Siebold publishes a book about animal-like microorganisms, which he calls protozoa.

1859 Charles Darwin publishes the first edition of *The Origin of Species*.

1866	Ernst Haeckel creates a separate kingdom for protists.
1930s	Edouard Chatton divides all living things into two groups: prokaryotes and eukaryotes.
1938	Herbert Copeland creates a separate kingdom for bacteria.
1950	Willi Hennig publishes a paper describing cladistics.
1953	James Watson and Francis Crick discover the structure of DNA.
1969	Robert Whittaker proposes a classification system with five kingdoms: plants, animals, fungi, bacteria, and protists.
1970	Lynn Margulis makes slight changes to Whittaker's five-kingdom classification system.
1977	Carl Woese proposes a six-kingdom classification system.
1990	Carl Woese proposes a three-domain classification system.
1996	A team of scientists led by Carol Bult sequences the genome of an archaea for the first time.
1998	Lynn Margulis and Karlene Schwartz publish the third edition of *Five Kingdoms: An Illustrated Guide to the Phyla of Life on Earth*.
2004	Scientists officially launch the Barcode of Life project.
2005	Researchers at the National Human Genome Research Institute finish sequencing the chimpanzee genome.
2007	The Barcode of Life project researchers announce the first successful study in mammals.

Biographies

Aristotle (384–322 b.c.) Aristotle was born in Stagira, Macedonia. At the age of seventeen, he began studying in Athens with a renowned teacher named Plato. When Plato died in 347 B.C., Aristotle moved to Assos, a city in Asia Minor (modern Turkey). He became a counselor to the ruler of Assos. In 345 B.C., Aristotle moved to Pella, the capital of Macedonia, and began tutoring the boy who became Alexander the Great, one of Greece's most important rulers. In 335 B.C., Aristotle returned to Athens and established a school of his own. In 323 B.C., Aristotle retired to a family estate. He died there the following year. Aristotle studied and wrote about physics, poetry, philosophy, psychology, logic, ethics, mathematics, government, and biology. He studied, described, and grouped hundreds of animals. He created a "ladder of nature" to show the relationships between the groups.

Charles Darwin (1809–1882) Charles Darwin was born in Shrewsbury, England. He studied medicine at Scotland's University of Edinburgh but dropped out after two years and began studying religion at Britain's University of Cambridge. During this time, Darwin became interested in nature and learned to be a careful, patient observer. After graduating in 1831, he sailed around the world on the *Beagle,* collecting samples and taking notes. Upon returning to Britain in 1836, Darwin quickly developed the basic ideas for the theory of evolution by natural selection, which he would describe in *The Origin of Species.* He announced his theory in 1858 in a paper presented alongside a similar one by Alfred Russel Wallace. Darwin published his complete theory in 1859, in *The Origin of Species,* and spent the rest of his life expanding on the book.

Ernst Haeckel (1834–1919) Ernst Haeckel was born and raised in Potsdam, Germany. He received a medical degree at the University of Berlin in 1857 but practiced medicine only briefly before teaching comparative anatomy at the University of Jena. After reading *The Origin of Species,* Haeckel promoted Darwin's ideas. Using them as a starting point, Haeckel tried to create a unifying theory of biology, which claimed that the steps of embryonic development retrace the steps of evolution. Later, Haeckel became interested in a group of microorganisms he called protists. He suggested that protists were so different from plants and animals that they should be considered a third kingdom of life. Haeckel also coined the term *ecology* and proposed that many of the unique features seen in male animals make them seem more attractive to potential mates. Haeckel died in Jena in 1919.

WILLI HENNIG (1913–1976) Born in Dürrhennersdorf, Germany, Willi Hennig volunteered at the Dresden Museum as a boy. This experience led to a career as a teacher and researcher at the German Entomological Institute. During World War II (1939–1945), he served as a soldier until 1942, when he was severely wounded and taken prisoner. After a long recovery, he worked in malaria prevention programs for Great Britain. By 1949 Hennig had returned to the German Entomological Institute. He was working there when he published his landmark paper describing cladistics. In 1961, when the Berlin Wall was built, Hennig could no longer travel from his home in West Berlin to the German Entomological Institute in East Berlin. He worked for a brief time at the Technical University of Berlin and then became the head of the new Department for Phylogenetic Research at the State Museum of Natural History in Stuttgart. Hennig was elected to the Royal Swedish Academy of Sciences, and he received the gold medal of the Linnaean Society and the gold medal of the American Museum of Natural History.

JEAN-BAPTISTE LAMARCK (1744–1829) Jean-Baptiste Lamarck was born in Bazentin-le-Petit, France. He initially attended a religious school, but after his father's death in 1759, he entered the military. In 1768 Lamarck began to study medicine and botany in Paris. He became an associate botanist in 1783, but he did his most significant work later at Paris's Muséum National d'Histoire Naturelle, where he was professor of insects and worms. Lamarck spent many hours studying and classifying the creatures he called invertebrates. He was one of the first scientists to write about evolution. His ideas had a big influence on Charles Darwin. Most of Lamarck's life was a struggle against poverty. Around 1818 he began to lose his sight. He spent his last years completely blind and penniless. He received a poor man's funeral and was buried in a rented grave.

CARL LINNAEUS (1707–1778) Carl Linnaeus was born into a religious family in a small town in rural Sweden. He inherited his father's love of plants. In 1727 he entered Lund University to study medicine but soon transferred to Uppsala University because it had a better botany program. As early as 1730, Linnaeus began developing a system for classifying plants. After plant-collecting journeys to Lapland and central Sweden, where he met his wife, Linnaeus traveled to the Netherlands to complete his medical education. In 1735 Linnaeus published *System of Nature,* which presented his new system for classifying plants, animals, and minerals. In later editions, he removed minerals and incorporated binomial nomenclature. In 1738 Linnaeus returned to Sweden and began practicing medicine. In 1741 Linnaeus began teaching botany at Uppsala University. He stayed there for the rest of his career, leaving only when his health failed in 1770. He died in 1778.

LYNN MARGULIS (B. 1938) Lynn Margulis was born in Chicago, Illinois. After graduating from the University of Chicago, she earned graduate degrees from the University of Wisconsin-Madison and the University of California, Berkeley. During graduate school, Margulis became interested in mitochondria. In 1967 she published a paper proposing that mitochondria and chloroplasts were once independent cells and that they fused with other cells to form the world's first eukaryotes. She published her version of the tree of life in 1970. In the early 1980s, she teamed up with Karlene Schwartz to write *Five Kingdoms,* which they published in 1982 and revised in 1988 and 1998. During this period, she also developed several important theories on the role of microorganisms in evolution. In 1989 Margulis took a position at the University of Massachusetts, Amherst. As of 2007, she has written more than two hundred scientific papers, nine scientific books, a dozen popular essays, and a novel. She was elected to the National Academy of Sciences in 1983 and awarded the National Medal of Science in 1999.

JOHN RAY (1627–1705) John Ray was born to a poor family in Black Notley, England. Scholarships enabled him to attend the University of Cambridge. Then, with money from a fellowship, Ray spent the next thirteen years teaching and collecting and cataloging plants. After he lost his fellowship for political reasons, friends and former students funded his work. Ray published many papers and is remembered for coining the terms *species, pollen,* and *petal;* dividing flowering plants into monocots and dicots; and suggesting the use of Latin scientific names. Perhaps most importantly, he proposed a classification system that emphasized looking at an organism as a whole. He used his system to organize more than eighteen thousand plant species. Ray's ideas had a big impact on Carl Linnaeus.

ROBERT WHITTAKER (1920–1980) Born in Wichita, Kansas, Robert Whittaker graduated from Washburn Municipal College and then served in the army during World War II. In 1948 he received a PhD from the University of Illinois. He became a teacher at Washington State College in Pullman and later worked for the Aquatic Biology Unit at Hanford Laboratories. In 1953 Whittaker took a job at Brooklyn College in New York City and began doing research at the New Jersey Pine Barrens. During this period, he developed a classification system that introduced the fungi kingdom. He also worked on a variety of forest ecology projects. After working at the University of California at Irvine and Brookhaven National Laboratory, Whittaker moved on to Cornell University, where he spent the rest of his career. He was elected to the National Academy of Sciences and the American Academy of Arts and Sciences. He served as vice president of the Ecological Society of America and president of the American Society of Naturalists.

CARL WOESE (B. 1928) Born in Syracuse, New York, Carl Woese received degrees in mathematics and physics from Amherst College. He earned a PhD in biophysics at Yale University. In 1960 Woese took a position as a biophysicist at the General Electric research laboratory. Woese left this post in 1964 to teach microbiology at the University of Illinois, where he continues to teach. Around 1970 Woese became interested in the evolution of translation, but before he could research this, he needed to understand the evolutionary relationships among bacteria. He spent several years analyzing the rRNA of nearly four hundred bacteria species so he could classify them. In 1977 he and microbiologist Ralph Wolfe realized that two very different kinds of bacteria exist. They suggested classifying what they called archaea into a sixth kingdom of life. Later, Woese decided that archaea are so different from both eubacteria and eukaryotes (eukarya) that life on Earth should be divided into three large groups called domains. Woese was elected to the National Academy of Sciences in 1988. In 1992 he earned microbiology's highest honor, the Leeuwenhoek Medal.

Source Notes

4 Mary Beckman, "Biologists Find New Species of African Monkey," *Science News*, May 20, 2005, 1,103.

10 Aristotle, "On the Parts of Animals, Book 4," *The Internet Classic Archive*, n.d., http://www.classics.mit.edu/ Aristotle/parts_animals.html (April 3, 2007).

18 Louise Petrusson, "Carl Linnaeus," *Swedish Museum of Natural History*, May 10, 2004, http://www2.nrm.se/fbo/ hist/linnaeus/linnaeus.html.en (April 3, 2007).

19 Elis Malmeström and A. H. Uggla, *Vita Caroli Linnaei. Carl von Linnaeus Autobiography* (Stockholm: Almquist & Wiksell, 1957), 90.

26 Charles Darwin, *The Origin of Species* (New York: Bantam, 1999), 1.

30 Charles Darwin, *The Origin of Species* (Cambridge, MA: Harvard University Press, 1964), 132.

32 Virginia Morrell, "Microbiology's Scarred Revolutionary," *Science*, May 2, 1997, 701.

SELECTED BIBLIOGRAPHY

Abbott, David, ed. *The Biographic Dictionary of Scientists: Biology.* New York: Peter Bendick Books, 1984.

Beckman, Mary. "Biologists Find New Species of African Monkey." *Science News,* May 20, 2005, 308.

Blunt, Wilifrid. *The Compleat Naturalist: A Life of Linnaeus.* London: Collins, 1971.

Brownlee, Christen. "DNA Bar Codes: Life Under the Scanner." *Science News,* December 4, 2004, 360.

Ellavich, Marie C. *Scientists: Their Lives and Work.* Detroit: UXL/Gale, 1999.

Goerke, Heinz. *Linnaeus.* New York: Charles Scribner & Sons, 1973.

Johnson, George B., and Peter H. Raven. *Biology: Principles and Explorations.* Austin, TX: Holt, Rinehart, and Winston, 2001.

Krause, David. Personal interview. February 15, 2002.

Malmeström, Elis, and A. H. Uggla, *Vita Caroli Linnaei. Carl von Linnaeus Autobiography.* Stockholm: Almquist & Wiksell, 1957.

Margulis, Lynn, and Karlene V. Schwartz. *Five Kingdoms: An Illustrated Guide to the Phyla of Life on Earth.* 3rd ed. New York: W. H. Freeman and Company, 1998.

Marshall, Eliot. "Will DNA Bar Codes Breathe Life into Classification?" *Science,* February 18, 2005, 307.

Milius, Susan. "New Mammals." *Science News,* May 21, 2005, 324.

Morrell, Virginia. "Microbiology's Scarred Revolutionary." *Science,* May 2, 1997, 699–702.

National Center for Biotechnology Information. "Systematics and Molecular Phylogenetics." *National Center for Biotechnology Information.* April 1, 2004. http://www.ncbi.nlm.nih.gov/About/primer/phylo.html (April 3, 2007).

Petrusson, Louise. "Carl Linnaeus." *Swedish Museum of Natural History*. May 10, 2004. http://www2.nrm.se/fbo/hist/linnaeus/linnaeus.html.en (April 3, 2007).

Sherman, E. J. "Robert H. Whittaker." *Biographical Memoirs*. Vol. 59. Washington, DC: National Academy of Sciences, 1990.

Than, Ker. "Scientists Discover New Monkey Genus in Africa." *LiveScience*. May 11, 2006. http://www.livescience.com/animalworld/060511_monkey_genus.html (April 3, 2007).

University of California Museum of Paleontology. "Carl Linnaeus." *University of California Museum of Paleontology*. N.d. http://www.ucmp.berkeley.edu/history/linnaeus.html (April 3, 2007).

Wade, Nicholas. "A Species in a Second: Promise of DNA 'Bar Codes.'" *New York Times*. December 14, 2004.

Wildlife Conservation Society. "Kipunji Facts." *Wildlife Conservation Society*. 2007. http://www.wcs.org/international/Africa/Tanzania/kipunji/kipunjifacts (April 4, 2007).

FURTHER READING

Anderson, Margaret J. *Carl Linnaeus: Father of Classification.* Springfield, NJ: Enslow, 1997.

Fleisher, Paul. *Evolution.* Minneapolis: Twenty-First Century Books, 2006.

Fridell, Ron. *Decoding Life: Unraveling the Mysteries of the Genome.* Minneapolis: Lerner Publications Company, 2005.

Johnson, Rebecca L. *Genetics.* Minneapolis: Twenty-First Century Books, 2006.

McGowen, Tom. *The Beginnings of Science.* Brookfield, CT: Millbrook, 1998.

Orenstein, Ron. *New Animal Discoveries.* Brookfield, CT: Millbrook, 2001.

Patent, Dorothy Hinshaw. *Charles Darwin: The Life of a Revolutionary Thinker.* New York: Holiday House, 2001.

Watson, James D. *The Double Helix: A Personal Account of the Discovery of DNA.* New York: Touchstone, 1968.

WEBSITES

Classification of Living Things: Introduction
http://anthro.palomar.edu/animal/animal_1.htm
Created and maintained by a biology professor at Palomar College in San Marcos, California, this site contains basic information about the reasons we classify life, the contributions of Linnaeus and Darwin, and the way modern scientists classify organisms.

Classifying Living Things
http://faculty.fmcc.suny.edu/mcdarby/Animals&PlantsBook/History/02-Explaining-Life-Classification.htm
This site was created and is maintained by the faculty of the State University of New York's Fulton Montgomery Community College. It provides a thorough background of the Linnaean classification system with some information about cladistics.

Kipunji
http://www.wcs.org/international/Africa/Tanzania/kipunji
This page on the Wildlife Conservation Society's website has photos and information about the kipunji. It also includes a map that shows where the monkeys live.

The Tree of Life Cladogram
http://ology.amnh.org/biodiversity/treeoflife/pages/cladogram.html
This explanation of cladograms and the tree of life was created and is maintained by the American Museum of Natural History.

Tree of Life Web Project
http://tolweb.org/tree/phylogeny.html
This gigantic website contains hundreds of pages that describe living and extinct organisms and show evolutionary trees that represent scientists' up-to-the-minute ideas about how the organisms are related. The pages are frequently updated as scientists learn more about living things and their evolutionary relationships.

What Did T. Rex Taste Like? An Introduction to How Life Is Related
http://www.ucmp.berkeley.edu/education/explorations/tours/Trex/index.html
Check out this site for a clear, simple explanation of cladistics and cladograms.

INDEX

Photo Acknowledgments

The images in this book are used with permission of:
© Tim Davenport/WCS, p. 7; © Jerome Wexler/Visuals
Unlimited, p. 13 (left); © Gustav W. Verderber/Visuals
Unlimited, p. 13 (right); © Archive Photos/Getty Images, p. 14;
© Hulton Archive/Getty Images, pp. 24, 28, 31; © Laura
Westlund/Independent Picture Service, pp. 20, 37, 38, 48, 53,
58; Library of Congress (LC-DIG-ggbain-05698), p. 36; © Dr.
Dennis Kunkel/Visuals Unlimited, p. 40 (left); © Science VU/
Frederick Mertz/Visuals Unlimited, p. 40 (right); © A.
Barrington Brown/Photo Researchers, Inc., p. 47; © Robert
Longuehaye, NIBSC/Photo Researchers, Inc., p. 54.

Cover: © Ken Lucas/Visuals Unlimited (top left); U.S. Fish
and Wildlife (top right); © Tim Parlin/Independent Picture
Service (illustration).